Dear Parent:

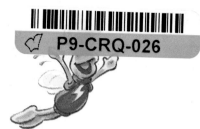

Congratulations! Your child is taking the first steps on an exciting journey. The destination? Independent reading!

STEP INTO READING® will help your child get there. The program offers five steps to reading success. Each step includes fun stories and colorful art. There are also Step into Reading Sticker Books, Step into Reading Math Readers, Step into Reading Write-In Readers, Step into Reading Phonics Readers, and Step into Reading Phonics First Steps! Boxed Sets—a complete literacy program with something for every child.

Learning to Read, Step by Step!

Ready to Read Preschool–Kindergarten
• big type and easy words • rhyme and rhythm • picture clues
For children who know the alphabet and are eager to begin reading.

Reading with Help Preschool–Grade 1
• basic vocabulary • short sentences • simple stories
For children who recognize familiar words and sound out new words with help.

Reading on Your Own Grades 1–3
• engaging characters • easy-to-follow plots • popular topics
For children who are ready to read on their own.

Reading Paragraphs Grades 2–3
• challenging vocabulary • short paragraphs • exciting stories
For newly independent readers who read simple sentences with confidence.

Ready for Chapters Grades 2–4
• chapters • longer paragraphs • full-color art
For children who want to take the plunge into chapter books but still like colorful pictures.

STEP INTO READING® is designed to give every child a successful reading experience. The grade levels are only guides. Children can progress through the steps at their own speed, developing confidence in their reading, no matter what their grade.

Remember, a lifetime love of reading starts with a single step!

www.stepintoreading.com

Educators and librarians, for a variety of teaching tools, visit us at
www.randomhouse.com/teachers

Library of Congress Cataloging-in-Publication Data
Ross, Katharine. Twinkle, twinkle, little bug / by Katharine Ross ; illustrated by Tom Brannon.
   p.   cm. — (Step into reading. A step 2 book)
SUMMARY: Big Bird captures a lightning bug and decides to keep it in a jar.
ISBN 0-679-87666-9 (trade) — ISBN 0-679-97666-3 (lib. bdg.)
[1. Fireflies—Fiction.   2. Birds—Fiction.]
I. Brannon, Tom, ill.   II. Title.   III. Series: Step into reading. Step 2 book.
PZ7.R719693 Tw 2003 [E]—dc21   2002013876

Printed in the United States of America   21 20 19 18 17 16 15 14 13 12

STEP INTO READING®

STEP 2

Twinkle, Twinkle, Little Bug

by Katharine Ross
illustrated by Tom Brannon

Random House New York

One night

Big Bird saw something

glowing in the dark.

"Look!" he said.

"A lightning bug!"

TWINKLE, TWINKLE, TWINKLE

went the lightning bug.

"Come here, little bug!
I won't hurt you,"
said Big Bird.
He put the lightning bug
in a jar.

TWINKLE, TWINKLE, TWINKLE

went the lightning bug.

"Ernie, look at my lightning bug," said Big Bird. "Twinkle for Ernie, little bug."

TWINKLE, TWINKLE, TWINKLE

went the lightning bug.

"Zoe, look at my
lightning bug,"
said Big Bird.
"Twinkle for Zoe,
little bug."

TWINKLE, TWINKLE, TWINKLE

went the lightning bug.

"Bert, look at my
lightning bug,"
said Big Bird.
"Twinkle for Bert,
little bug."

But the lightning bug
would not twinkle.

"Why won't you twinkle,
little bug?"
asked Big Bird.

"Maybe he's lonely,"

said Bert.

Big Bird talked to
the little bug
so he would not be lonely.

But the lightning bug
would not twinkle.

17

"Maybe he's tired,"
said Elmo.

Big Bird gave
the lightning bug
a pillow
so he could
take a nap.

But the lightning bug
would not twinkle.

"Maybe he's hungry,"
said Cookie Monster.

Big Bird gave the
lightning bug one of
Cookie Monster's
cookies to eat.

But the lightning bug
would not twinkle.

"Maybe he wants
to hear some music,"
said Hoots the Owl.

Hoots played some jazz.
Big Bird joined in.
"Twinkle, twinkle,
little bug!"
sang Big Bird.

But the lightning bug
still would not twinkle.

"Grover, why won't
my lightning bug twinkle?"
asked Big Bird.
"I talked to him.
I gave him a pillow
to sleep on.
I gave him a cookie to eat.
I played music for him.
I am his friend!"

"Would you twinkle
if you were
stuck in a jar?"
asked Grover.
"Gee," said Big Bird,
"I guess not."

Big Bird opened the jar
and set the little bug free.
"Twinkle, twinkle,
little bug!"
said Big Bird.

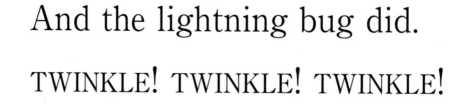

And the lightning bug did.

TWINKLE! TWINKLE! TWINKLE!